Little Bear's
Alphabet

JANE HISSEY

RED FOX

a b c d e f g h i j k l m

Aa

A is for animals. All the animals are asleep
except Little Bear.

Sleep!

n o p q r s t u v w x y z

B b

B is for box. Bramwell Brown has a big box
of buttons.

Pick up box
Tip it up
what fell out of your box!?

a b c d e f g h i j k l m

Cc

C is for cake. Bramwell is cutting a piece for Camel.

Cut a piece for your partner - pass it on, eat it up!
Yum. mine is cool!

D is for doll. She is wearing a blue dress and hat.

Hold your doll - mine is called Daisy. Daisy Doll.
Whats yours called?

a b c d e f g h i j k l m

E e

E is for egg. Be extra careful, Little Bear.
Please don't drop it.

Lets eat an egg! Put it in the egg cup. Cut of
the top part! Scoop it out - Don't drop it!

n o p q r s t u v w x y z

F is for food. This picnic food looks fun to eat.

a b c d e f g h i j k l m

G g

G is for game. The toys are playing a game of hide-and-seek. Can you find them?

Pretend you are hiding.
Are you behind / under / inside something. Be very quiet!

H h

H is for holding on. Hold on tight, Little Bear,
Hoot is flying high.

Lets be   hoot!   Put Little bear (Bean bags)

a b c d e f g h **i** j k l m

I is for inside. Little Bear is inside his sleeping bag.

J j

J is for jelly. Don't jump in Ruff's birthday jelly,
Little Bear.

a b c d e f g h i j k l m

K is for kangaroo. She is kicking a big red ball.

L l

L is for leaf. Don't let go, Little Bear.

a b c d e f g h i j k l **m**

Mm

M is for marbles. How many marbles has Cat found?

Nn

N is for nest. Hoot's new nest is a nice woolly hat.

O is for on. Old Bear is sitting on top of a basket watching Little Bear.

Pp

P is for present. This one is wrapped in pretty paper.

a b c d e f g h i j k l m

Q is for quiet please. Old Bear is sleeping under his quilt.

n o p q r s t u v w x y z

R r

R is for run. Rabbit is running in a race.

S s

S is for sand, small stones and a spade.

Tt

T is for tent. These two friends are camping
in the garden.

a b c d e f g h i j k l m

U u

U is for upside down. There are four bricks under
Little Bear.

V v

V is for vase. That's not a very good hiding place, Rabbit!

a b c d e f g h i j k l m

W is for wool. I wonder what Bramwell Brown
is knitting?

n o p q r s t u v w x y z

Xx

X is for xylophone. Duck is playing some music.

a b c d e f g h i j k l m

Yy

Y is for yellow. Can you see two yellow ducks?

n o p q r s t u v w x y z

Z z

Z is for Zebra. What is she pulling in her little red cart?

Some letters make new sounds
when they are side by side.

Ch

Ch is for choose. Little Bear has chosen a chalk to write with.

Sh

Sh is for shadows. Little Bear is showing Rabbit
his shadow picture on the wall.

Th

Th is for things. What letters do the things on the shelves begin with?

For Di

Old Bear and Friends by Jane Hissey in Red Fox

OLD BEAR
LITTLE BEAR'S TROUSERS
LITTLE BEAR LOST
JOLLY TALL
JOLLY SNOW
RUFF
HOOT
OLD BEAR AND HIS FRIENDS
OLD BEAR TALES
LITTLE BEAR'S DRAGON

A Red Fox Book

Published by Random House Children's Books
20 Vauxhall Bridge Road, London SW1V 2SA

A division of The Random House Group Ltd
London Melbourne Sydney Auckland
Johannesburg and agencies throughout the world

Text and illustrations copyright © Jane Hissey 1986,
1987, 1988, 1989, 1990, 1992, 1994, 1996, 1999, 2000

1 3 5 7 9 10 8 6 4 2

First published in Great Britain by Hutchinson Children's Books 2000
Red Fox edition 2001

The right of Jane Hissey to be identified as the author and illustrator
of this work has been asserted by her in accordance with the
Copyright, Designs and Patents Act, 1988.

Printed and bound in Singapore

THE RANDOM HOUSE GROUP Limited Reg. No. 954009

www.randomhouse.co.uk

ISBN 0 09 940857 0